PLACES AND PEOPLE

The Indian Subcontinent

Anita Ganeri

Franklin Watts

New York • Chicago • London • Toronto • Sydney

© 1994 Franklin Watts

Franklin Watts
95 Madison Avenue
New York, NY 10016

10 9 8 7 6 5 4 3 2 1

Ganeri, Anita.
The Indian Subcontinent/Anita Ganeri.
p. cm. – (Places and people)
Includes index.
ISBN 0-531-14272-8
1. India – Economic conditions – 1947 – Juvenile literature.
2. India – Social conditions – Juvenile literature. [1. India.]
I. Title. II. Series.
HC435.2.G287 1994
954 – dc20   94 – 3970
                                                          CIP
                                                          AC

Series consultant: Anna Sandeman
Editor: Jane Walker
Design: Ron Kamen, Green Door Design Ltd
Cover design: Mike Davis
Maps: Mainline Design
        Visual Image
Additional artwork: Mainline Design
                        Visual Image
Cover artwork: Raymond Turvey
Fact checking: Simone K. Lefolii
Research: Jonardon Ganeri
Picture research: Alison Renwick

Cover photographs: left, Supreme Courts, Lahore, Pakistan (Christine Osborne Pictures);
center, Street dwellers in Delhi, India (Christine Osborne Pictures); right, Karakoram
Highway, Pakistan (Christine Osborne Pictures).

Photographic credits: (t = top, m = middle, b = bottom): Associated Press 13(t); J. Allan
Cash 11(m), 16(b); Colorific! 5(m) Penny Tweedie; Chris Fairclough Colour Library 7(b),
8(b), 25(b); Robert Harding Picture Library 14, 17(m) G. Hellier, 22(b) David Lomax,
23(m), 25(m) Duncan Maxwell; Jim Holmes 5(t) Royal Geographical Society, 6, 7(t),
13(b), 15(b), 16(t), 18, 19(b), 21(m), 22(t); Hutchison Library 17(b) N. Durrell McKenna,
25(t), 26(b) Christine Pemberton, 27 Liba Taylor, 29; Christine Osborne Pictures 7(m),
8(t), 10, 11(t), 15(t), 19(m), 21(t), (b), 23(b), 26(t); Frank Spooner Pictures 5(b)
Bartholomew/Liaison, 9 Bartholomew/Liaison, 32 Bartholomew/Liaison.

Artwork credit: The village plan on p.17 is based on a plan originally reproduced
in *India: Paths to Development*, published by Oxfam.

Printed in Belgium

Contents

Where is the subcontinent?

The Indian subcontinent covers some 1.5 million square miles (4 million sq km) of the southern part of Asia, the world's largest continent. The area is often referred to as South Asia. It includes the countries of India, Pakistan, Bangladesh, Sri Lanka, Nepal, and Bhutan. It is fringed by the Indian Ocean, the Arabian Sea, and the Bay of Bengal. The subcontinent is a vast area, where at least one-fifth of the world's people live. This huge and rapidly growing population is one of the subcontinent's most serious problems. The land and natural resources will simply not be able to support too many more people.

The map on the left shows the countries that make up the Indian subcontinent. India dominates the region because of its size.

Islamabad

PAKISTAN

New Delhi

NEPAL

Thimphu

Kathmandu

BHUTAN

BANGLADESH

Dhaka

INDIA

BAY OF BENGAL

The Indian subcontinent is located in the southern part of Asia, the world's largest continent.

ARABIAN SEA

N

ASIA

0	500	1000 km
0	300	600 miles

SRI LANKA

Colombo

INDIAN OCEAN

After independence

With the exception of Nepal and Bhutan, most of the subcontinent formed part of the British Empire in the nineteenth and early twentieth centuries. India and Sri Lanka (formerly Ceylon) both regained their independence in the 1940s, when the new country of Pakistan was also created. Bangladesh came into being in 1971.

Since gaining their independence, all these countries have been trying to develop their economies and societies. The people are mostly poor by Western standards. Efforts are being made to improve their standards of living. Improvements in agriculture and industry have been particularly successful.

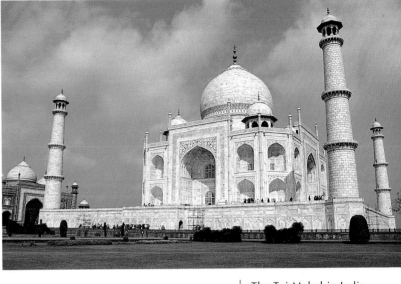

The Taj Mahal in India was built in the seventeenth century by the Mughal emperor Shah Jahan as a memorial for his wife. It is one of the subcontinent's most visited landmarks.

Heavy flooding is a regular problem in the low-lying coastal areas of Bangladesh (left). In 1992, Pakistan's worst floods in decades left at least 2,000 people dead and around 3 million homeless.

Religion is another driving force behind life and current events on the subcontinent. Long-standing rivalry between Hindu and Muslim groups in India, for example, continues to make the headlines. In the early 1990s, religious violence broke out in the town of Ayodhya (below) in India. Fanatical Hindus destroyed a Muslim mosque.

Regional images

For 4,500 years, the Indian subcontinent has been a major center of civilization. It has been invaded many times, mainly along its northwest borders. As a result, today it is a melting pot of many different influences. Among the people of the subcontinent there are many different cultures, beliefs, and languages.

The geography of the subcontinent also affects the images of the region that we see in the news. For example, in 1992, serious flooding occurred in Pakistan and Bangladesh after local rivers had burst their banks.

A vast landscape

The Indian subcontinent is, in fact, a separate physical region. The hard crust around the earth is divided into a number of huge sections, called plates. Over millions of years, these plates have drifted on top of the layer of liquid rock beneath them. In this way, the size and position of the Earth's continents have changed.

The Indian subcontinent is part of the Indo-Australian plate and was once attached to Australia. It moved northward and crashed into the Eurasian plate about 40 million years ago. The seabed between the two plates was pushed upward by this massive collision, forming a great range of mountains, called the Himalayas. These mark the northern boundary between the subcontinent and the rest of Asia. The two tiny kingdoms of Nepal and Bhutan lie among the Himalayas.

This map shows the physical geography of the Indian subcontinent, including its major mountain ranges, rivers, and plains.

N

| 0 | 500 | 1000 km |
| 0 | 300 | 600 miles |

HINDU KUSH

Jhelum

Indus

THAR DESERT

HIMALAYAS

Mt Everest (8,848 m)

INDO-GANGETIC PLAIN

Ganges

Brahmaputra

Meghna

Narmada

DECCAN PLATEAU

WESTERN GHATS

Godavari

EASTERN GHATS

Mahaweli

Kelani

mountainou

lowland

desert

major river

This mountainside fortress stands in the Himalayas near Mustang in Nepal. The mountain range includes the world's highest mountain, Mount Everest (29,028 feet/8,848 m), which stands on the border between Nepal and Tibet.

A varied geography

The vast subcontinent has a very varied landscape, ranging from snowcapped mountains to tropical rain forest, to sandy desert. There are four major geographical areas. In the north lie the Himalayas and other mountains. The Himalayas are the world's highest mountains, with more than 80 peaks over 24,605 feet (7,500 m) high. To the south is the triangular-shaped part of India, known as peninsular India. In the west, the Thar Desert covers an area of about 100,000 square miles (250,000 sq km). Lastly, the Indo-Gangetic Plain stretches from the Indus River in Pakistan right across India to the part of the Ganges Delta that is in Bangladesh. Here the river flows into the Bay of Bengal. Ninety percent of Bangladesh's surface is taken up by the delta area of the Ganges and Brahmaputra rivers.

View across the Thar Desert from Kot Diji in Pakistan. The desert reaches from the western Indian state of Rajasthan across the border into eastern Pakistan.

The south coast of Sri Lanka is lined with sandy beaches and fringed with tropical palm trees.

Life along the rivers

The first great civilization on the subcontinent flourished along the banks of the Indus River, in what is now Pakistan, in 2500 B.C. It was known as the Indus Valley Civilization.

Rivers play an important role in the subcontinent today. The Indo-Gangetic Plain is one of the most densely populated regions in the world. Its fertile soils support about half the population of the subcontinent. As the Ganges River flows out into the Bay of Bengal, it deposits islands of silt in the delta. These islands are very fertile and attract many farmers, despite the risk of flooding and cyclones in this area (see page 9).

The Indus River was the lifeblood of the ancient civilization that grew up in its valley. Farmers grew crops in the rich, silty soil, which was deposited when the river flooded. The downfall of the Indus people in about 2000 B.C. may have been caused by a combination of serious floods and changes in the river's course, which left the valuable farmland dry and infertile.

Monsoons and seasons

The Indian subcontinent has a wide range of climates. In India, for example, rainfall varies considerably. While parts of the western desert receive less than 2.6 inches (6.5cm) of rain a year, in the northeast 788 inches (20m) of rain may fall each year. Average temperatures range from about 50°F to 104°F (10°C to 40°C). Bangladesh has a tropical monsoon climate, while the climate of Pakistan is generally hot and dry. In the far south of the subcontinent, Sri Lanka has a tropical climate. In the far north, the climate in Nepal and Bhutan becomes colder as you reach higher up in the mountains.

It is unbearably hot in parts of India during the hot season. Some of the highest temperatures are recorded on the northern plains. Thunderstorms herald the beginning of the wet season.

The mighty monsoon

The Indian climate is dominated by monsoon winds. The term "monsoon" refers to winds that change direction according to the time of year. The monsoon blows from the southwest in summer, then changes direction and blows from the northeast in winter. The southwest monsoon is the most important of the two. It arrives in India in June, bringing torrential rain — about two-thirds of the country's annual rainfall. India's farmers rely on the monsoon rains to water their crops and ensure a good harvest. In a largely agricultural society like India's, the failure of the monsoon spells disaster.

In northern India the monsoon divides the year into three seasons — wet, cool, and hot. The rains end in September, bringing the wet season to a close. The cool season lasts from October through February. January is the coolest month of the year, with temperatures dropping to about 50°F (10°C). In March, the hot season begins and the temperature rises quickly. May is the hottest month. Temperatures can rise to over 113°F (45°C) in some areas. In southern India temperatures are hot all year round.

Temperatures in the mountains begin to fall the higher up you go. On the mountain-tops, it is always so cold that the ice never melts.

8

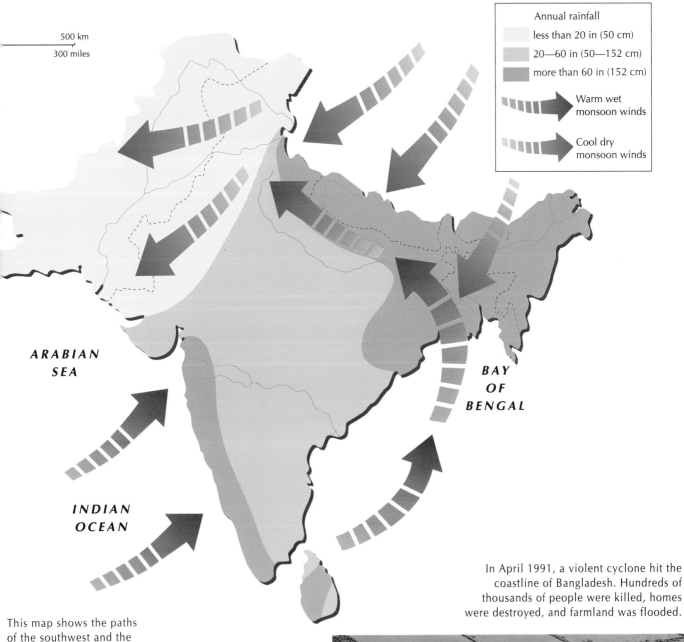

500 km

300 miles

*ARABIAN
SEA*

*INDIAN
OCEAN*

*BAY
OF
BENGAL*

This map shows the paths of the southwest and the northeast monsoons, as well as the annual rainfall across the subcontinent.

In April 1991, a violent cyclone hit the coastline of Bangladesh. Hundreds of thousands of people were killed, homes were destroyed, and farmland was flooded.

Weather extremes

Too much or too little rain means loss of food and income for the subcontinent's farmers. Flooding is common in the delta region of Bangladesh. This area also suffers devastating tropical storms, called cyclones, at the end of the wet season. If the rivers do not flood, no fertile silt is deposited to enrich the soil in which the farmers grow their crops. Yet if the floods are too heavy, any crops are quickly washed away.

Peoples and population

The Indian subcontinent is one of the most densely populated areas on Earth. After China, India is the world's most populous country, with over 880 million people, or around one in five of all the people in the world. The population of the whole subcontinent is about 1,130 million. This number is expected to rise by about 2 percent a year. India's population is likely to reach 1 billion by the year 2000. At present, over 25 million babies are born each year in India. Family planning is now an essential part of the subcontinent's future.

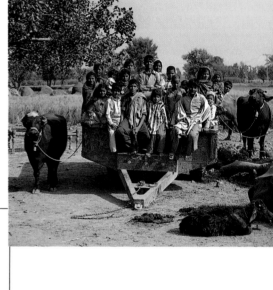

Children in a Punjabi village, Pakistan.

Life expectancy

One of the reasons that people have so many babies on the subcontinent is the high death rate among babies and young children. About one in ten babies dies before its first birthday. People also have large families because parents rely on their children to share their workload and take care of them in old age. Life expectancy is about 58 years in India but only 48 to 50 years in Bhutan.

0   800 km
0   500 miles

Indus
Delhi
Ganges
Brahmaputra
Dhaka
Calcutta
Bombay
Godavari

Low density

High density

N

The map shows the distribution of the population of the Indian subcontinent. People are not spread evenly throughout the region. More people live along the Ganges, Indus and Brahmaputra rivers, and along the coasts, than anywhere else.

This tribal woman comes from Goa in western India. The traditional way of life of many *adivasis* (original people) is threatened by the exploitation of the natural resources found in their forest homes.

People and origins

The physical appearance of the people on the subcontinent tends to vary according to the region they come from. People from the south and east are usually shorter and darker skinned than people in the north. Regional differences can also be seen in the types of food that people eat and in the clothes they wear.

In India, there are about 400 tribal groups. Most live in central and eastern India. They are known as *adivasis*, which means "original people." They have lived in the forests, hunting and gathering food, for thousands of years. Today, however, their forest homes are being cleared to provide lumber or to gain access to mineral resources. Some forest areas have been flooded during the building of large dams.

A wealth of languages

A wide range of languages is spoken across the subcontinent. Hindi is the national language of India, although it is mainly spoken in the north of the country. India also has 14 other official languages, 13 of which correspond to different states. There are hundreds of regional dialects.

English is widely spoken throughout the subcontinent. Urdu is the national language of Pakistan, and Punjabi is widely spoken there too. In Bangladesh, 95 percent of the people speak Bengali, having once been part of the Indian state of Bengal. Sinhalese and Tamil are the national languages of Sri Lanka, reflecting the large number of Tamils living on the island. (Tamil is also the language of Tamil Nadu, the southernmost state of India.) Nepali is the national language of Nepal. It is also spoken by about one-quarter of the population of Bhutan, who are settlers from Nepal. Bhutan's official national language is called Dzongkha. It is written in Tibetan script.

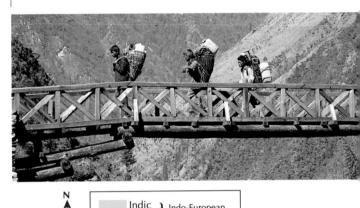

The Sherpa people of Nepal respect the mountains as the homes of the gods. The Sherpas themselves are respected as excellent climbers, able to carry heavy loads even at high altitudes.

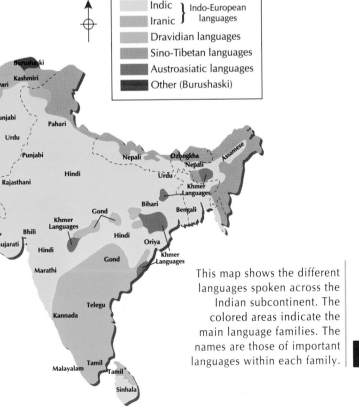

This map shows the different languages spoken across the Indian subcontinent. The colored areas indicate the main language families. The names are those of important languages within each family.

Indic ⎫ Indo-European
Iranic ⎭ languages
Dravidian languages
Sino-Tibetan languages
Austroasiatic languages
Other (Burushaski)

From colonial past to present-day independen[ce]

Although the Indian subcontinent is now made up of several independent countries, during the nineteenth and early twentieth centuries most of the region was part of the British Empire. In 1612, the British East India Company set up its first trading post in India at Surat on the coast of Gujarat. By 1690, it also had trading posts in Madras, Bombay, and Calcutta, around which these present cities grew up.

At first, British interest in the subcontinent lay only in trade. By the mid-nineteenth century, however, the British had political control of most of India. (At that time, India included modern-day Pakistan and Bangladesh.) In 1858, the British crown took over control of India from the East India Company and in 1877, Queen Victoria became empress of India. Until 1947, India remained part of the British Empire.

This map shows the extent of British India before 1947, and the boundaries created by the division of India in 1947. In 1971, India declared war on Pakistan in support of East Pakistan's claim to be an independent country. East and West Pakistan were separated by some 990 miles (1,600 km) of Indian territory.

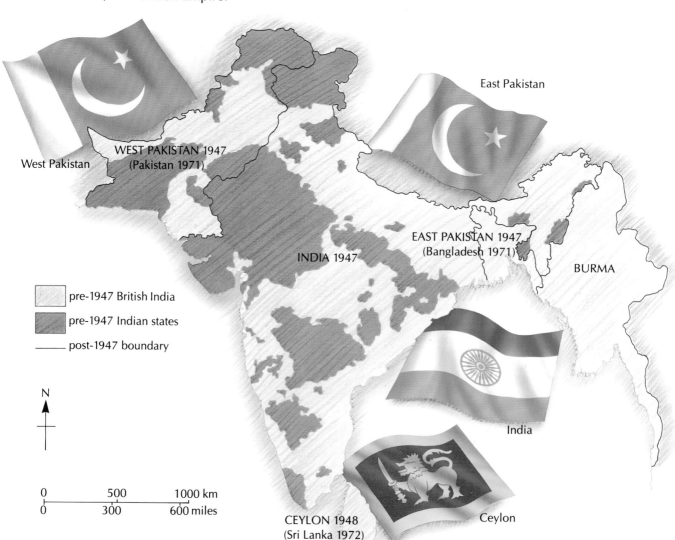

East Pakistan

WEST PAKISTAN 1947
(Pakistan 1971)

West Pakistan

EAST PAKISTAN 1947
(Bangladesh 1971)

BURMA

INDIA 1947

pre-1947 British India

pre-1947 Indian states

——— post-1947 boundary

N

India

CEYLON 1948
(Sri Lanka 1972)

Ceylon

0	500	1000 km
0	300	600 miles

Dividing India

In 1947, India gained its independence from Britain. However, the country was split into mainly Hindu India and mainly Muslim Pakistan. But it could not be divided neatly in two. The majority of India's Muslims lived in the western state of Punjab and the eastern state of Bengal, on opposite sides of the country. The new boundaries were drawn through these two states to create West Pakistan and East Pakistan.

The result of the division, or partition, of India was chaos. The man-made boundaries dividing India and Pakistan left millions of people displaced and homeless. For months afterwards, refugees fled in both directions across the new borders, in fear for their lives if they stayed behind. Around 10 million people moved from India to Pakistan and from Pakistan to India. Many were massacred while fleeing from one country to the other. In 1971, East Pakistan became the independent country of Bangladesh.

Muslim refugees in 1947 crowd onto a train bound for Pakistan. They are fleeing from the New Delhi area of India.

Trouble spots

Religious differences are the main reason for the remaining trouble spots on the subcontinent. India and Pakistan are still in dispute over the northern state of Kashmir. At the time of India's independence, Kashmir had a mainly Muslim population. However, the state was ruled by a Hindu maharaja who chose to belong to India. Following recent outbreaks of violence, the Indian Army has sent thousands of troops to the region.

Other trouble spots include the Indian state of Punjab where many Sikhs are demanding their own state, to be called Khalistan. In Sri Lanka, a Tamil terrorist group, called the Tamil Tigers, has been responsible for violence and bloodshed, including the assassination of the country's president, Ranasinghe Premadasa, in May 1993.

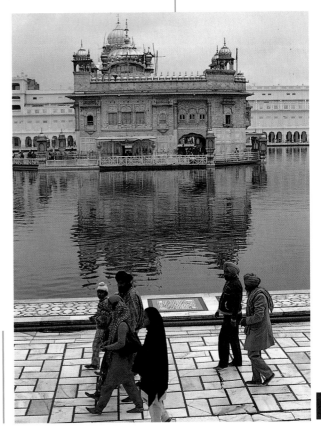

The Sikh Golden Temple in Amritsar in the Indian state of Punjab. Following the partition of India in 1947, Punjab's two major cities, Lahore and Amritsar, were separated from each other. Lahore became part of West Pakistan while Amritsar remained in India.

Regions and religions

The most important factor determining how people on the Indian subcontinent live, where they live, and even what they eat, is religion. India was partitioned along religious lines; current trouble spots across the subcontinent are largely the result of religious differences. Yet the vast majority of people live together peacefully, whatever their religion.

Followers of seven of the world's major religions — Hindus, Muslims, Buddhists, Christians, Sikhs, Jains, and Parsis — live on the Indian subcontinent. About 83 percent of the people in India are Hindus. The state religion of Pakistan and Bangladesh, and the very reason for the creation of these countries, is Islam.

The religions of the Indian subcontinent also play an important part further afield. Many Hindus, Sikhs, and Muslims have emigrated from South Asia, taking their religious beliefs and customs with them. In many Western cities, Muslim mosques, Hindu temples, and Sikh *gurudwaras* (temples) are now built alongside Christian churches and Jewish synagogues.

N

| Hinduism |
| Islam |
| Buddhism |
| Sikhism |
| Christianity |
| Jainism |
| Tribal religio |

Amritsar
Indus
Haridwar
Himalayas
Ayodhya
Mathura
Lumbini
Yamuna
Allahabad
Sarnath
Ganges
Varanasi
Bodh Gaya
Ujjain
Narmada
Dwarka
Godavari
Krishna
Kanchipuram

Sacred place
Sacred river
Sacred moun

This map shows the distribution of the principal religions of the subcontinent, together with some of the most sacred sites.

These pie charts show the breakdown of the various religions in four of the subcontinent's countries. Hinduism is the region's dominant religion. (See map, above right, for the color key to the religions.)

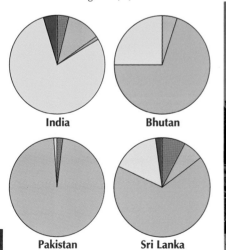

India

Bhutan

Pakistan

Sri Lanka

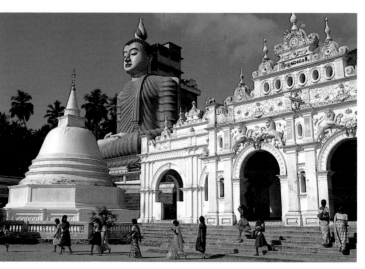

A Buddhist templ and statue of the Buddha, Sri Lanka. Buddhism was founded in India in about 50(B.C. It is now the major religion of Bhutan and Sri Lanka.

Sacred places

Many places on the subcontinent, as well as general geographical features such as mountains and rivers, are considered to be sacred. Millions of pilgrims visit these places each year. Hindus believe that the Himalaya mountains are the home of one of their most important gods, Shiva. At the time of the full moon in July–August, thousands of people make the *yatra* (pilgrimage) to the Sri Amarnath Cave in the foothills of the Himalayas in Kashmir. Here they worship at a natural ice shrine dedicated to Shiva.

The city of Allahabad lies in northern India at the meeting place of the Ganges and Yamuna rivers. This meeting place is believed to be particularly good for washing away sins. Every 12 years a special bathing festival, called the Kumbha Mela, is held here. A huge campsite is set up for the millions of pilgrims who attend. A smaller festival is also held here each year.

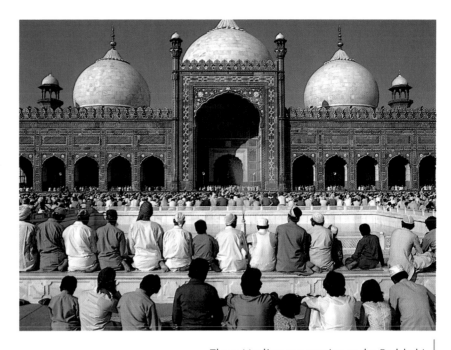

These Muslims are praying at the Badshahi Mosque in Lahore, Pakistan. Each year Muslim pilgrims leave the subcontinent for their most important pilgrimage – the hajj – to Mecca, in Saudi Arabia. Every Muslim who can is supposed to make the journey at least once in his or her lifetime. Mecca is the birthplace of the prophet Muhammad, the founder of Islam.

Benaras, or Varanasi, in northern India is the holiest city of the Hindus. It lies on the banks of the Ganges River. For Hindus, the Ganges is a sacred river. Bathing in its water is believed to wash away a person's sins. Pilgrims bathe from a series of steps, called *ghats*, leading down into the river.

15

Rural life

About four-fifths of the total population of the Indian subcontinent live in villages dotted about the countryside. The majority make their living by farming the land. There are some 580,000 villages in India, alone. Some are more like small towns than villages; others are tiny.

Village life

Village houses are made from local materials, such as mud bricks, covered with more mud and cow dung. Cow dung is also dried and used as fuel for the cooking fires. In remote regions, such as the mountains, many villages do not have facilities such as electricity or running water. Many villagers are very poor. The average villager has only a tiny plot of land to cultivate. This has to provide food for his family and to sell at market. Many villagers do not own their land. They have to rent it from landlords, who may take a proportion of what they grow instead of money. Many villagers are treated unfairly by landlords. Some villagers work as daily laborers on other people's land. But such work is scarce once the harvest is over.

This Hindu family in Bangladesh have made their house from bamboo, with a roof of corrugated iron.

Rural mosque in Sunamganj, Bangladesh. Many villages have temples or mosques, together with small roadside or household shrines.

Life in villages throughout much of the subcontinent is largely traditional. In many places, it has not changed much for hundreds of years. Villages are still very lively places. There are fairs and festivities to celebrate events in the farming year, such as plowing and harvesting, and special occasions, such as weddings. Even those people who leave their villages to look for work in the big cities maintain strong links with their homes. They regularly send money home and return whenever they can. They also tend to marry people from their own villages or districts.

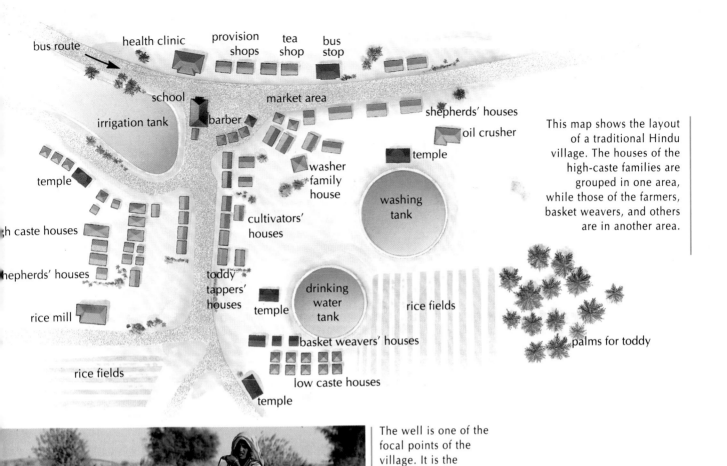

bus route
health clinic
provision shops
tea shop
bus stop

school
market area
irrigation tank
barber
shepherds' houses
oil crusher
temple

temple
washer family house
washing tank

h caste houses
cultivators' houses

hepherds' houses
toddy tappers' houses
drinking water tank
temple
rice fields

rice mill
temple
basket weavers' houses
palms for toddy

rice fields
low caste houses
temple

This map shows the layout of a traditional Hindu village. The houses of the high-caste families are grouped in one area, while those of the farmers, basket weavers, and others are in another area.

The well is one of the focal points of the village. It is the women's job to collect water each day.

Family life

All over the subcontinent, family life is extremely important. Many people live in extended families, that is, children, parents, grandparents, aunts, uncles, and cousins all live together under one roof. From an early age, children help their parents in the fields and with household tasks such as cooking and fetching water from the village well. Some children may attend the village school, which is often held outdoors. Many village families cannot afford to let their children go to school for long, however. They need their help in earning a living.

These children are being taught by a village elder in an informal outdoor school.

17

Farming and food

In every country of the Indian subcontinent, except Sri Lanka, at least half of the workforce is involved in farming. In Nepal and Bhutan, this figure rises to more than 90 percent. Farms are mostly small and traditional. Most are used for subsistence farming, which means farming for food. More than 50 percent of the land in India as well as 65 percent of the land in Bangladesh is farmed.

Terraced fields like these in Nepal are cut into the mountainsides. By doing this, it is possible for farmers to grow rice on steep, inaccessible land.

Agriculture relies heavily on the monsoon rains, and the types of crops grown reflect the climate. Rice is one of the main crops grown and eaten on the subcontinent. It thrives in the wet conditions. In a drier country like Pakistan, however, where rainfall is low and unreliable, irrigation is essential. Other major food crops include wheat, maize, potatoes, sugarcane, spices, fruit, and legumes (lentils, chickpeas, etc).

Food for thought

The types of food that the people eat vary according to where they live and what religion they follow. Along the coasts, people eat fish. Meals are accompanied by rice, in the rice-growing areas of southern India, or bread, in the wheat-growing north.

This chart shows the daily calorie intake of people living on the Indian subcontinent compared with that of people living in the United States and the United Kingdom.

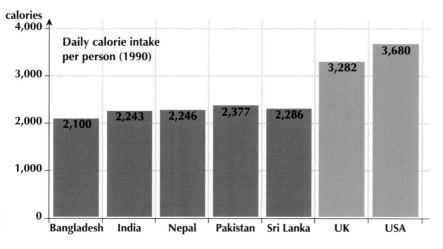

Daily calorie intake per person (1990)

Country	calories
Bangladesh	2,100
India	2,243
Nepal	2,246
Pakistan	2,377
Sri Lanka	2,286
UK	3,282
USA	3,680

Many Hindus are vegetarians, and most never eat beef. Hindus consider cows to be sacred animals. Muslims do not eat pork, which they consider to be unclean. The majority of people cannot afford a particularly healthy diet. In Bangladesh and Bhutan, not enough food is produced to feed everyone properly. In Nepal and Bhutan, the problem is made worse by the hilly, inhospitable land, which makes farming difficult and time consuming.

This map shows the major food crops grown on the Indian subcontinent. India produces over 90 percent of the region's legumes and 75 percent of its rice.

N

| 0 | 500 | 1000 km |
| 0 | 300 | 600 miles |

rice

corn

wheat

sugarcane

millet

legumes

The Green Revolution

One of the great struggles that faces farmers on the subcontinent is that of producing enough food for the growing populations of their countries. In the past, food production could not keep up with demand, and some countries had to import expensive food supplies. However, one of India's major successes since independence in 1947 has been its progress toward self-sufficiency in regard to food production. The Indian government also has large quantities of grain in storage, to prevent famine if harvests fail. The reason for this success was the so-called Green Revolution of the late 1960s. Higher-yielding types of wheat and rice seed were developed, and the use of fertilizers was increased.

These farmers are growing wheat in the Punjab, northern Pakistan. Across the border in India, the state of Punjab is known as the "granary of India" because of the huge amounts of wheat grown there.

Surplus fruit and vegetables are sold at daily or weekly markets like this one at Matara on Sri Lanka's south coast.

Farming for export

Many of the crops that are grown for use within the Indian subcontinent are also grown as crops for export. The major export crops are cotton, jute, tea and cardamom, and other spices. It was India's spices, as well as its brightly colored silks and satins that attracted European traders to South Asia in the sixteenth and seventeenth centuries. The export crops are sent to other countries within the subcontinent and further afield.

India

India's main export crops are cotton, tea, rice, cashew nuts, and spices. It also produces large quantities of groundnuts, sugarcane, coffee, leather, and some jute for export. India's main export partners are the Commonwealth of Independent States, the United States, Japan, the United Kingdom, and Germany.

This map shows where the subcontinent's major export crops are grown, as well as the principal export crops of the four larger countries. The figures are percentages of each country's total exports.

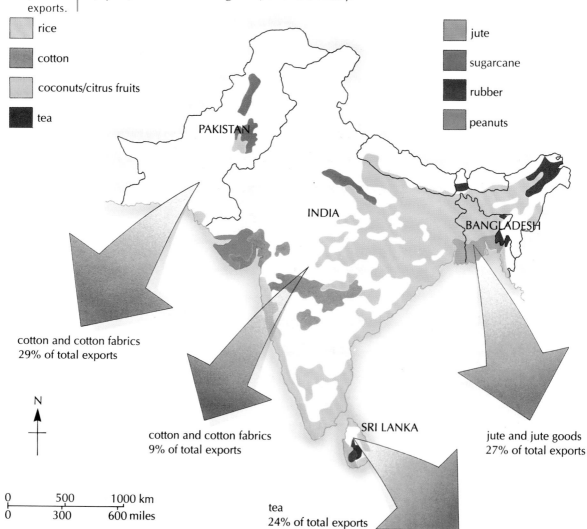

rice

cotton

coconuts/citrus fruits

tea

jute

sugarcane

rubber

peanuts

PAKISTAN

INDIA

BANGLADESH

cotton and cotton fabrics
29% of total exports

N

cotton and cotton fabrics
9% of total exports

SRI LANKA

jute and jute goods
27% of total exports

tea
24% of total exports

0	500	1000 km
0	300	600 miles

Pakistan

Cotton and rice are Pakistan's major export crops. Pakistan also exports fish and leather. It exports cotton in its raw state, as cotton thread, as fabric, and as ready-made clothes. Pakistan exports these items to the United States, Japan, Germany, the United Kingdom, and Saudi Arabia.

Bangladesh

Bangladesh's most important export crop is jute. This is a crop that flourishes in the damp climate and soils of its delta lands. When Bengal was partitioned in 1947, the jute mills and port remained on the Indian side of the dividing line, while East Pakistan was left with plenty of jute but not a single mill for processing it. Bangladesh also exports fish and leather to the United States, Italy, the United Kingdom, Singapore, and Germany.

Tea pickers on a plantation near Nuwara Eliya in Sri Lanka. The areas of Assam and Darjeeling in India are also famous for their tea plantations.

Sri Lanka

In 1990, Sri Lanka surpassed India as the world's top exporter of tea. It also exports rubber, coconuts, and precious stones such as sapphires and rubies to the United States, Germany, the United Kingdom, Japan, and Iran. Many of Sri Lanka's export crops are grown on huge plantations rather than on smallholdings.

These workers in Bangladesh are stripping bark from the stems of jute plants. The stringy fibers of the jute plant can be used to make rope, twine, and burlap.

Nepal

Jute, leather, and legumes are Nepal's main export crops. They are exported to India, Germany, the United States, Belgium, and the United Kingdom.

Bhutan

Bhutan is one of the world's biggest producers of cardamom spice. Lumber and fruit, especially oranges, are other important export crops. Over 90 percent of Bhutan's export crops are sent to India.

Cotton is the most important fiber grown for export. Like rice, it is a crop that needs to be kept well-watered. This cotton has been harvested in the Sind Province of Pakistan. India is now the world's fourth largest producer of cotton, after the United States, China, and the Commonwealth of Independent States.

21

Handicrafts and heavy industry

Since Indian independence in 1947, industry throughout the subcontinent has expanded quickly. India, for example, now ranks among the world's top 12 industrialized nations in terms of the quantity of goods produced. However, it is not just major industries such as engineering or iron and steel production that are important. Small-scale industries, including family-run handicraft businesses, are responsible for about half of India's industrial output. These so-called "cottage" industries are vital to the economies of all the countries on the subcontinent.

A Nepalese woman weaves cloth outside her home. Fewer than 5 percent of Nepal's population work in industry.

Handicrafts

Handicrafts from the Indian subcontinent are sold all over the world. These are largely produced by traditional village businesses in which skills are handed down from one generation to the next. Traditional methods of textile design include embroidery, block printing, mirror work, and tie-dye. Other forms of handicraft include carpets and papier-mâché goods from Kashmir, basketwork from Nepal, statues carved from fragrant sandalwood or cast in bronze, and exquisite jewelry made from locally mined gold and precious stones.

Natural resources

Industry relies on natural resources. The subcontinent has a wide range of mineral resources but they are not divided evenly between all of its countries. India has huge stocks of iron ore and coal, which have enabled it to develop a thriving steel industry. About 12 million tons of steel are produced each year. Steel is used to make cars, bicycles, and motorcycles. One of India's most heavily industrialized areas lies around the city of Jamshedpur in the Damodar Valley near Calcutta. Because of its position near major iron ore and coal deposits, it has become a center of iron and steel production.

Steelworks at Jamshedpur, India.

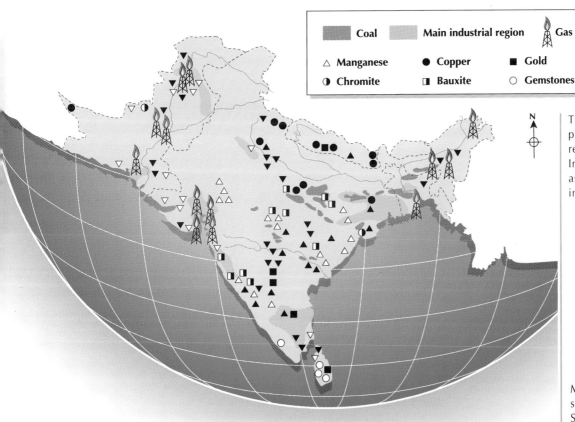

This map shows the principal mineral resources of the Indian subcontinent, as well as its main industrial regions.

Mining precious stones at Ratnapura, Sri Lanka.

Pakistan's main mineral export is oil. Chromite, limestone, and rock salt are also mined. Large quantities of gemstones are mined in Sri Lanka and exported abroad. Bangladesh has very few natural resources apart from natural gas. The textile industry is a major source of its foreign earnings. It has to import fuel, metals, and machinery. Talc is Bhutan's main export mineral but it has reserves of other minerals, such as limestone and dolomite, which have not yet been fully exploited.

Water power

The mighty rivers of the subcontinent are able to provide some countries with cheap and plentiful hydroelectricity. Hydroelectric power provided by fast-flowing mountain rivers is the principal energy resource of Sri Lanka, Nepal, and Bhutan. In 1986, the Chukha hydroelectric project was launched in Bhutan to provide inexpensive electricity for use at home and for export. Pakistan has also been able to produce valuable hydroelectricity from its three major rivers – the Indus, the Jhelum and the Kabul.

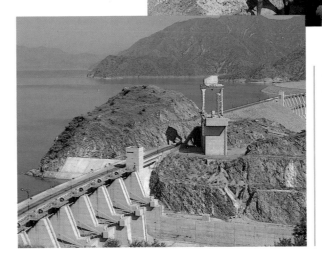

This dam at Tarbela near Rawalpindi, Pakistan, is the world's largest earth-filled dam. About half of Pakistan's electricity comes from hydroelectric power stations.

Help for the environment

Many of the illnesses suffered by people on the subcontinent are carried by water. These water-borne illnesses include typhoid, hepatitis, cholera, diarrhea, and dysentery. They are often fatal.

As the subcontinent has developed its industry and agriculture, serious damage has been done to its environment. Smoke, fumes, and discharge from factories have polluted the air and water.

Dirty air and water

Many of the subcontinent's biggest cities suffer from serious air pollution, caused mainly by smoke and fumes from factories and cars. Levels of poisonous gases such as sulfur dioxide in Calcutta and Bombay are above the safe limits set by the World Health Organization.

Very few towns throughout the subcontinent have adequate sewage systems. Human waste (together with animal waste and factory runoff) is often dumped right into the nearest river. As a result, many of the region's most important rivers, such as the Ganges, the Indus, and the Narmada, are severely polluted. About one-quarter of the total length of the Ganges River is so polluted that it has become a health hazard. The Central Ganges Authority was set up in 1985 to clean up the river and organize the building of new sewage treatment plants. Its task is an enormous one.

Clearing the forests

Soil erosion and deforestation are becoming widespread. Forests are being destroyed at an alarming rate for fuelwood, to clear space for mines, and for the building of huge hydroelectric and irrigation dams. One of the largest schemes is the vast irrigation and dam project along India's Narmada River.

In India, local conservation groups are now working with the government to protect the environment. A massive reforestation program has been set up to plant millions of new trees.

On December 3, 1984, poisonous gas leaked from the Union Carbide pesticide factory in Bhopal, India. It killed over 2,000 people and injured hundreds of thousands more in the nearby shantytowns. Many of these people died later.

This map shows the locations of the subcontinent's most polluted rivers and of its national parks.

Indus

Luni

Ganges

Brahmaputra

Narmada

Mahanadi

Godavari

Krishna

Tungabhadra

Kaveri

national park

main river

polluted stretch of river

Bhopal

| 0 | 500 | 1000 km |
| 0 | 300 | 600 miles |

Protecting wildlife

The Indian subcontinent has over 2,000 species of birds and 500 species of mammals. Today, many of these creatures are very rare. The main threat to their existence is the destruction of their natural habitats, as forests are cut down and lakes and rivers become polluted. In some areas, wild animals come into conflict with local people, as, for example, when elephants raid farmers' crops.

National parks have now been established all over the region to protect endangered animals, such as tigers, rhinoceroses, lions, macaques, storks, and deer. Whole regions are protected, too. About one-fifth of Bhutan has been designated as a nature reserve because of its outstanding natural beauty.

In India, 15 nature reserves were established in 1973 as part of Project Tiger. The project aimed to save the Indian tiger from extinction. Since 1900, tiger numbers had dropped from thousands to hundreds. They have now begun to rise again, and there are between 3,000 and 4,000 tigers in India.

The Sundarbans is the world's largest mangrove forest. It stretches over thousands of square miles across the Ganges Delta in India and Bangladesh. The area is an important spawning ground for fish and shellfish, and therefore provides local people with work. The mangrove trees also help to protect the coast from damage by cyclones.

Cities and crowds

The majority of people on the subcontinent live in the countryside, although the urban population is growing fast throughout the region. This is mainly due to the large numbers of people who come to the cities from the countryside in search of work. Bombay is the biggest city on the subcontinent, with some 12.5 million inhabitants in the metropolitan and surrounding areas. The population of Calcutta, the subcontinent's second largest city, has doubled in the past 40 years.

About one-fifth of city dwellers live in slums or shantytowns, or even on the streets, like this family.

City life

The cities of the subcontinent are mostly crowded, bustling places. Overloaded buses share the packed streets with rickshaws, honking cars, taxis, people, and even sacred cows! People from the countryside may get jobs as rickshaw or taxi drivers, in hotels, or as servants to wealthy families. Many live in crowded shantytowns or slums, often with no access to clean water or to sewage facilities. Outbreaks of diseases such as typhoid and dysentery are common in these places. In some cities, the authorities have now accepted that the shantytowns are there to stay, and are trying to improve conditions for the people living in them.

A view of Bombay shows the contrast between modern high-rise buildings and the shantytowns of the poor.

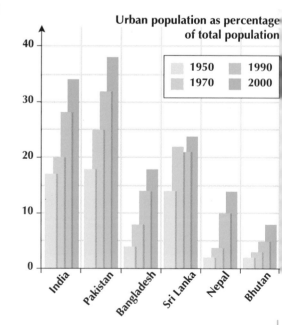

Urban population as percentage of total population

Key: 1950, 1970, 1990, 2000

Chart showing urban population percentages for India, Pakistan, Bangladesh, Sri Lanka, Nepal, and Bhutan.

This chart shows how much the urban population has increased over the past 40 years, and its projected increase into the year 2000.

The transportation system

The cities of the Indian subcontinent are linked by a vast transportation network. Travel is possible by air, rail, bus, car, bullock cart, and if you live in the desert, by camel. India has the fourth largest railroad system in the world. The British had the first tracks laid in the mid-nineteenth century, to make it easier to travel around and to govern India. The railroads also helped to unite the country by linking remote villages. Today there are more than 38,750 miles (62,500 km) of track, and the railroads carry about 3.5 billion passengers each year.

Travel abroad

In the nineteenth and early twentieth centuries, many people from India (which then included present-day Pakistan and Bangladesh) traveled abroad to work on European sugar, coffee, tea, and rubber plantations. They were poorly paid, and often badly treated. Since independence in 1947, hundreds of thousands of Indians have left the subcontinent to live and work abroad. Many have gone to the United Kingdom; others have settled in the West Indies and the Middle East.

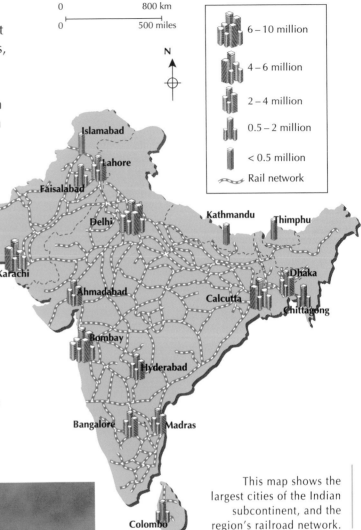

This map shows the largest cities of the Indian subcontinent, and the region's railroad network.

A crowded passenger train in Tamil Nadu, southern India.

Looking forward

The countries of the Indian subcontinent face many problems as they look toward the future. They must try to control the increase in their populations. Also, they must work toward improving health and welfare services. They must also try to resolve the conflicts between members of different religious and ethnic groups. These conflicts threaten the stability of areas of the subcontinent. Governments have already begun to tackle some of these problems.

This map shows member countries of the Commonwealth of Nations and of the Non-Aligned Movement.

Non-Aligned Movement
Commonwealth of Nations

World affairs

The Indian subcontinent plays an important role in world affairs. India, Pakistan, Bangladesh, and Sri Lanka are members of the Commonwealth of Nations. This is an association of most of the former colonies of the British Empire. They are all equal partners, with the British queen as the nominal head of the Commonwealth. All the countries of the subcontinent belong to the Non-Aligned Movement (NAM). The NAM is not linked politically to either the United States or the Commonwealth of Independent States. The countries of the subcontinent also belong to the South Asia Regional Co-operation Organization (SAARC).

Local people in Jodhpur, India, listen to an election speech. India is the world's most populous democracy.

Facing the future

Bangladesh

The People's Republic of Bangladesh is one of the poorest countries in the world. Its problems in the future include trying to grow enough food to feed its people. In addition, Bangladesh regularly has to cope with major natural disasters, such as cyclones and serious floods.

Bhutan

Bhutan has close political links with India. In 1990 there were violent demonstrations against the Bhutanese government by Nepalese settlers living in the south of the country. The unrest continues.

India

The future problems of this huge democracy include continuing population growth and repeated outbreaks of violence between Hindus and Muslims. However, India has made great strides in the fields of science and technology, including space and agricultural research.

Nepal

Following protests for a more democratic government, Nepal has been ruled by an elected government since the early 1990s. There is still political unrest in the country, and many people are desperately poor. Nepal has renewed its trade links with India, hoping to improve its economic situation. Recently, it has become a popular tourist destination for trekkers and climbers.

Pakistan

The Islamic Republic of Pakistan has had a turbulent political history since independence in 1947. Political unrest continues in Pakistan, together with religious and territorial conflicts with India. Pakistan has an important role to play as one of the leading nations of the Indian subcontinent.

Sri Lanka

Sri Lanka's most urgent problem is to resolve the conflict between the government and a terrorist group called the Tamil Tigers. The group claims to represent the rights of the minority Tamil population in Sri Lanka. The Tamils originally came from the southern Indian state of Tamil Nadu.

Databank

Physical geography

- The Himalayas are between 95 and 250 miles (150 and 400 km) wide, and 1,550 miles (2,500 km) long from northwest to southeast. Only 14 of the world's mountains are over 8,000 metres high, and all 14 are in the Himalayas.
- The world's land areas were once all joined together in a giant supercontinent called Pangaea. About 200 million years ago Pangaea began to split in two, and by 80 million years ago India had broken away from Australia and Antarctica. It then began to move northward.
- The amount of rainfall divides Sri Lanka into two distinct regions: the Wet Zone in the southwest, and the Dry Zone which covers the rest of the island.
- People in Tamil Nadu, the most southerly state in India, are more than 1,240 miles (2,000 km) away from the Indian capital, New Delhi. That is about the same distance as between London and the city of Athens in Greece.

People

- India was the first country in the world to have a national family planning program. It was set up in 1952.
- About 40 percent of people in the Indian subcontinent are below the age of 15.
- More children work in India than in any other country. They are mostly children from poor rural areas whose parents need them to help in the fields as well as in the home.
- The population of the Indian subcontinent between 1950 and 1990, and the estimated population figures for the year 2000:

country	population (millions)					
	1950	1960	1970	1980	1990	2000 (est.)
India	350.4	431.5	551.3	689.06	844.0	1,041.5
Pakistan	40.0	50.1	63.7	87.1	113.1	162.4
Bangladesh*	42.3	51.6	66.7	88.2	118.0	150.6
Sri Lanka	7.7	9.9	12.5	14.8	17.2	19.4
Nepal	8.2	9.4	11.5	14.9	19.1	24.1
Bhutan	0.7	0.9	1.0	1.3	1.5	1.9
* East Pakistan until 1971						

Religion

- When a Muslim baby is born, the call to prayer is whispered into the baby's right ear and the start of prayer into the left ear. The baby is named seven days later, in a ceremony called the *aqiqah*.

- According to tradition, Sikh men must wear or carry five signs of their religion. These are known as the five "K." They are *kes* (uncut hair and beard), *kangha* (a comb), *kirpan* (a dagger), *kara* (a steel bangle), and *kachh* (shorts).
- All Sikh men have the title "Singh" (Lion), and all Sikh women the title "Kaur" (Princess).

Language and education

- Hindi is the official language of India. It is the fourth most widely spoken language in the world.
- India has the third highest number of students in higher education in the world, after the United States and the Commonwealth of Independent States.
- Many students study religious texts and subjects such as language, philosophy, mathematics, logic, and astronomy.
- In Bhutan, tuition, textbooks, uniform, and board and lodging if necessary, are provided free of charge in primary schools. This is to encourage pupils to attend school.

Environment

- One of the best-known environmental groups in India is the Chipko Andolan (the Chipko Movement). Its aim is to save India's forests from destruction. The movement began in the early 1970s when a group of village women hugged nearby trees to stop them from being cut down.
- India's forests are being destroyed at a rate of 363,000 acres (147,000 ha) each year.
- It is estimated that about 73 million working days are lost in India each year through water-borne illnesses such as cholera and typhoid.

Politics

- India has an electorate of more than 450 million people (1988).
- The main political parties in India are: the Indian National Congress, the Janata Dal (a coalition party), the Communist Party, and the BJP (Bharatiya Janata party).
- The Indian constitution allows seats in the parliament building to be reserved for the scheduled castes (who used to be known as the "untouchables") and for the tribes.
- Bhutan's head of state is the king, who is called the Druk Gyalpo. In the villages, decisions affecting the local population are taken by the village headmen.
- Three countries of the Indian subcontinent have had women prime ministers: India (Indira Gandhi), Pakistan (Benazir Bhutto), and Sri Lanka (Sirimavo Bandaranaike).

Glossary

batik
A method of making patterns on cloth by using wax.

calorie
A measurement that tells how much energy is contained in different foods.

cardamom
A type of spice used in many of the subcontinent's dishes.

cyclone
A powerful tropical storm that brings heavy rain and strong winds. Cyclones can cause terrible destruction and loss of life. They are a type of hurricane.

delta
An area of low-lying land that forms where a river flows into the sea.

family planning
Different methods that are used to reduce the number of babies that are born each year.

fold mountain
A mountain that was formed when two pieces of the earth's crust crashed into each other. The crust between them was pushed up into gigantic folds.

hydroelectric power
Electricity which is made from the energy produced by fast-moving water.

irrigation
Taking water from rivers and dams to farmland where it is needed. The water is moved from place to place along canals, channels, and pipes.

life expectancy
The average number of years that a person can expect to live.

monsoon
A wind that blows across Asia and changes direction according to the time of the year. It can bring heavy rains.

natural resource
Any material which is found naturally in a country, such as coal, water, forests, fish, etc.

partition
Another word for division.

plate
One of the large pieces of the outer layer, or crust, that surrounds the earth.

refugee
A person who is forced to leave or flee their country because of war, famine, or unrest.

rickshaw
A two-wheeled vehicle which is used for transporting people and goods.

self-sufficiency
Self-sufficiency in food means that a country can grow and produce enough food to feed its people, without having to import food from other countries.

silt
Rich, fertile soil that is deposited by a river.

subcontinent
A huge area of land which is already part of a continent. A subcontinent can be as big as an actual continent.

tie-dye
A way of creating a pattern on cloth by tying the cloth with string and then dyeing it.

Index